The Glass Cat Eye

H.L. RANDALL

The Glass Cat Eye
H. L. Randall

Universal Battles Books RPG
703 W. Main Street
Alliance, Ohio, 44601
Universalbattles.com
412-586-8759

First published by Universal Battles Books RPG 2014

ISBN 978-0-9862928-5-9

Dedication

This book is dedicated to my son, Warren, for his suggestions and contributions to this writing project and to Babatunji for his encouragement and support.

Acknowledgement

I would like to thank Firstediting editor, Vonda for her valuable contribution to my manuscript. My appreciation also goes out to my graphic designer, Andrei Bat, (eze.graphics@yahoo.com) for this unique and exciting book cover. Finally, I would like to thank Pamela of Delaney-Designs for the lovely interior design of my book.

Contents

Chapter One

THE SÉANCE

(Dayton, Ohio)

Holding hands at the round table as Iris Keller responded to the voice of her dead lover made Steven Crane feel incredibly stupid. He was an atheist and believed that any claim on the supernatural had as much value as a bucket of warm piss. He had agreed to sit in on the séance just to humor his childhood friend, Esther West, a preacher's daughter who he felt had been duped right along with other ghost-believing idiots. Not that he thought that of Esther; he respected and loved her too much.

Outside, the lightning flashed and the thunder growled like a ferocious bear in combat. The September wind shook the house like it wanted in, and the rain beat hard against the windows. Large branches snapped like twigs and disappeared in the distance.

Inside, Madame Reece went deeper into her trance as the room grew dark and eerie. A lit candle placed in the middle of the table formed a hedge of protection around them—the flames dancing above the wick. Madame Reece's dark irises rolled to the back of her head and remained there. Blood trickled down from one ear as she foamed at the mouth like a rabid dog.

Creaking noises rose throughout the house, and thumping sounds moved along the walls. The six guests gripped each other's hands as a mist crept over the table and the ghostly face of a man formed out of the air. Steven felt Esther's hand tremble. She squeezed his hand until the blood slipped to his fingertips and made them thump with every beat of his heart. The muffled sound of a crying child loomed above the mist. One guest swore it was the voice of her little girl who'd drowned years ago. Another guest acknowledged an unknown person seated with them at the table; they all gasped when its presence vanished as quickly as it had appeared.

Steven's eyes scanned for hidden mikes, strings on flying objects, or black-clothed figures lurking in the background. But technology had become too sophisticated for an amateur psychic buster like him, he reasoned.

Esther appeared frightened, yet eager for the experience. Her request was next. Her deceased granny had moved up in the spirit line, or so she was told. Steven's eyes ping-ponged back and forth between Esther and Madame Reece. She no sooner had taken a hard swallow when Madame Reece screamed in multiple voices and collapsed. Steven wanted to stand and applaud the performance, but knew he'd be slaughtered by disapproving eyes. The lights flashed on, nearly blinding the guests. An assistant begged everyone's forgiveness. She announced that the session had ended, as another assistant escorted a weak Madame Reece from the room.

The séance left Steven quite amused; he wanted to hang back and ask them how they had produced the multiple voices, the facial aging and the blood coming from her ear. He couldn't believe this happened right in front of him. There seemed nothing but blank walls in the room and no tablecloth on the wooden table; nothing seemed hidden. Madame Reece was good, there was no doubt about that, he thought. Now what to do about Esther? The glow on her face told him everything; he definitely had his work cut out for him. Walking to their cars on the parking lot, she turned to him.

"So, what did you think?"

He said, "It's fake. You knew I'd say it."

"Yes, I knew, but you can't prove it."

"It was over too soon. We had stuff worked out."

"You mean all those lies you wanted me to feed her, to trip her up."

"Hell yeah, I wanted to trip her phony ass up. That was the plan. But I'll get my chance at the next session."

"I'm not inviting you to another session. I've had it with your damn skepticism. Just stay away from me." Esther turned and walked briskly ahead of Steven.

"Now you're being childish," he said, trying to catch up to her.

Esther stopped, then turned to him. "Childish? Maybe I am," she said. "Children tend to be open-minded to the unknown, don't they? And aren't we encouraged to be as little children when we read the Bible?"

"And what about what the Bible says about psychics? You can't just pick and choose what you want to believe."

"Like you don't?"

"What?" he asked, hunching his shoulders.

"If my father knew you questioned most of what he preaches, you wouldn't be allowed to step foot in our home, and you know it."

"I've never questioned his integrity. I just think he's bamboozled like the rest of religious society."

Her eyes widened when she looked at him. "My father? Bamboozled?"

"I can't help it if I don't buy your father's philosophy on hell fire and demons."

"Can't you just be a friend and support me?"

"I *am* your friend. That's why I won't stand by and watch you give hundreds of dollars to some crook who claims to conjure up your dead grandma. I'm sorry—but that's just plain stupid."

"Now I'm stupid?"

"I...I didn't say..."

"Fine!"

She turned sharply in stiletto heels and headed for her car. He reached for her. "Don't be like that. We've known each other forever. Kindergarten, children's church. Damn!"

Esther eluded his grasp. She slammed the door in his face and drove off. Steven was visibly shaken. He hated that this incident had come between them. But how, he thought, could he prove that Madame Reece was a phony? He fastened his seat belt and started the car. He knew if he were to put even a dent in this psychic scam, he had to do some digging into Reece's past and maybe snoop around her place too. As he left the parking lot, he seemed rather pleased with himself for what he'd planned. He drove off with his lips drawn in a devilish smile.

*****

(3:00 a.m.: the next Morning)

Madame Reece Weatherbee, or Reecie as she was called by those closest to her, lifted her head from her pillow and felt a slight pulling at her scalp. She examined the pillow and saw her dark brown strands pasted in dried blood. She touched her neck and felt the roughness of the tiny red crumbs that sprinkled down onto her shoulder. Madame had performed as a psychic most of her thirty-nine years. She never married, had no children and had lived on her own since age seventeen.

Reece walked to the bathroom and stood in front of the mirror. Her eyes looked like the "Before" Clear Eyes eye drop commercial. Her hair was matted and blood oozed from her left ear. A sharp pain rippled through her right arm when she reached for the shower knob. She stumbled back onto the toilet seat and tried to gather herself. A rap on the bedroom door startled her.

"Yes," she called out in a weak voice.

Debbie, a plump woman in her forties and one of Reece's assistants, walked into the bathroom where Reece sat. She playfully scolded Reece for not calling for help. Then she took cotton balls and Q-tips, dipped them in a solution and cleaned away the dried blood from Reece's ear and neck. She massaged her right arm, drew her bath and washed her hair. Madame Reece sat drying her hair with a towel while Debbie changed the bedding. Reece was exhausted.

"The spirits have been extremely demanding and unpredictable," she told Debbie.

Her bleeding ear, a preexisting condition made worse when using her gift, proved too painful to continue last night's session. Groggy from the pain medication her assistant had given to her, Reece slipped between the fresh covers and fell asleep; Debbie sat in a large armchair and monitored her every breath.

*****

(Private Study)

Dr. Richard D. Connelly squeezed the bridge of his nose between his forefinger and thumb for the seventh time after pulling off his glasses. He rubbed his tired blue eyes, yawned and took a sip of his sixth cup of black coffee. Joyce, his wife of twenty-eight years, was used to this by now. Their three kids, Palmer, JT and Brittany, had gotten used to it years ago, just before going off to college.

Joyce often put a snack on his nightstand and kept a light on in the hall so he wouldn't stumble on his way to bed. On his desk were a wave of notes and papers and a spread of books: *Conversations with the Other Side* by 19th century authors, *Beware the Lies of Satan* by Dr. Frederick K. C. Price, *The Study of Demonology* by various authors, *Why the Ouija Board is not a Kid's Game* by none other than Dr. Richard D. Connelly and piles of other references.

Dr. Connelly earned a PhD in Theology and had a passion for research on world religion. He was an academic expert, author of nine books and a valuable contributor of information about religious topics, including the occult; before retiring, he had been in great demand lecturing at top universities all over the world. But when he seemed affixed to just lecturing on the occult, he received scrutiny from his colleagues and admirers. They accused him of being too self-absorbed with, what they called, *this satanic thing,* and he was soon removed from their list of lecturers. His phone stopped ringing, and his touring dried up.

Fortunately, he had come from a financially secure family, and he had invested his own money well. This allowed him the finances and the freedom to continue to research and write books on his new subject. But it wasn't his fascination with the occult that influenced him and set him on this course; it was an earlier encounter that rocked his intellectual genius and changed his life's purpose forever.

It was 1993 in Blue Ridge, Ohio, a conservative town—population 743—where Dr. Connelly was lecturing at a small Bible college. In the middle of his lecture, he noticed a young female, not seated with the others, but standing off in a dark corner of the auditorium. Her disheveled appearance, dark scrawny face, and deep disturbing eyes set her apart from the rest of the audience. Her wool scarf was wrapped several times, which seemed much too tightly, around her tiny neck. She looked about seventeen. She wore a dark wool cap pulled down over long, stringy, dirty blonde hair; the long-sleeved pink sweater she wore was pulled over her hands, covering her finger-tips.

She folded her arms across her chest, held each shoulder with the opposite sweater-covered hand and rocked back and forth. With her head bowed, she glared up at him with eyes as black as coal, with no white showing. He tried not to notice her, but her glare seemed to hypnotize him; no matter where he looked out over the crowd, his eyes were drawn back to her. Suddenly their glares locked, and a cold wind swept over the stage that chilled him until he nearly gasped. He lost focus on his lecturing and had to struggle to resume. But what she did next sent a sharp jolt through every nerve in his body; first he saw her, then the wall through her, then just the wall. He played it off by reaching for a drink of water and clearing his throat.

After the lecture, Dr. Connelly was still shaken and acting noticeably strange. His colleague and friend, Professor Bob Wilder, who had invited him to lecture, confronted him; he asked him what was wrong. When Dr. Connelly told him, he was quite surprised that Professor Wilder's facial expression never changed, nor had he appeared frightened. Professor Wilder asked him into his private office. "Have a seat, Richard. I keep this for special occasions." Professor Wilder poured the imported wine into two glasses and handed one to Dr. Connelly. He sat across from Connelly and crossed his legs. Then Wilder told him a haunting story about how quiet the town had been until a group of psychics came to set up a new meeting ground.

"Right away, people complained about seeing this strange looking girl," he said. "But it was soon discovered it wasn't a girl at all, but a demon who'd taken possession of a dead girl's body."

"Just when did you know it was a demon?"

"When the psychics who had survived it came to us—scared out of their freaking minds, apologizing and warning us about what they had done."

"So *they* were responsible?"

"Oh hell yeah. Once they'd realized their mistake, they tried to send it back; but the damn thing didn't want to go back. So it killed the lot of 'em. Their bodies were so torn apart, we couldn't tell who was who, or what body parts went where…"

"Holy Christ!" Dr. Connelly blurted.

"…so we shoveled what we could find into one big bloody meat pile and gave them a Christian burial. Don't know who their families were."

"And the dead girl?"

"Nobody knows that either."

"Why couldn't they send it back? And where did it come from?"

"We don't know and we really don't talk about it much. The only reason I'm telling you now is because I had an idea what had happened to you out there on the stage; I felt I owed you an explanation. So please don't ask me anymore."

"You saw what happened to me out there and weren't going to say anything?"

"Well, I'm saying it now, aren't I?"

Dr. Connelly shook his head. "But…this thing—surely it must make you uneasy, popping in and out, scaring people. How do you live with it?"

"We leave *it* alone and it leaves *us* alone."

"Sure, it leaves your town folk alone. But what about outsiders like me? Why did it come to me? You know I nearly freaked out on that stage."

"That's another reason why I broke my silence, to give you this warning…I don't know why it came to you. Perhaps it feels threatened by you. Maybe because of your religious practice, I'm not sure. But I know from experience that it's not a good sign, and if I were you, I'd leave town immediately."

After all Dr. Connelly had heard, his heart was thudding. He thanked his colleague for the warning and promised after learning all he could about this strange phenomenon, he'd be back someday to deal with it.

That was over fifteen years ago, and Dr. Connelly still struggled to make good on that promise. He had spent the past eight years contacting mediums and warning them about the danger of their practices. He wasn't interested in shutting down psychic businesses that were scamming people out of their money. He left *that* to law enforcement. He was only interested in the mediums who actually contacted the demonic world.

He had been studying this evil for years and had become expert on understanding their strengths and weaknesses. The psychics were tapping into an unknown force that was about to turn the world to chaos of apocalyptic proportions. He had to warn them that one of them could just be one séance away from unleashing this unholy terror.

Dr. Connelly had sent out letters to various psychics asking for a meeting; he hoped the meeting would help get a better understanding of each other's position, but many feared it was just a trick for him to know who they were so he could attempt to stir up trouble for them. Only a few were gracious enough to respond. The doctor read one such letter from Madame Reece, agreeing to meet with him. He was very pleased.

*****

(A small town in Cleveland)

Steven shifted himself a few times in the large beige chair but never got comfortable. He finally leaned forward, sitting wide-legged, placing an elbow on each knee, and folded his hands in front of him. The thick blue carpet swallowed his feet as his eyes darted back and forth, taking in the well-kept beauty of the room in Madame Reece Weatherbee's childhood home.

Katherine Weatherbee-Dawson, Reece's mom, was widowed for the second time. She tried to make small talk, and Steven strained to hear her over the constant clinking of the dishware as she prepared two cups of spice tea. Mrs. Dawson had been reluctant to talk with a stranger about her daughter. But something in the way she wasn't too eager to stop the conversation either prompted Steven to push for a face-to-face meeting.

Katherine kept in touch with her daughter even though they weren't close anymore. Everything was fine as long as Katherine kept off the subject of what Reece was doing with her life. Reece called it a gift; Katherine had a more sinister name for it.

Steven examined the wall of pictures–one of a little girl, about six, in a blue and white school uniform. She had dark hair and big brown puppy eyes, with a smile that lit up a room. Another showed her cheek-to-cheek with a red-headed man.

"I love that one," Katherine said. Steven turned around, and she handed him the cup of tea. "That's Reecie and her father." She gestured to Steven to take a seat beside her on the over-stuffed multi-colored sofa.

He sat and crossed his legs. "How old was she?" Steven wasn't exactly a 'tea' person. He politely took a sip and placed the cup and saucer on the glass table.

"Eleven. But he died just weeks before her twelfth birthday."

"He was ill?"

"No. It was a sudden heart attack."

"That must have hurt Reece terribly."

"It did. She was never the same after that. God knows I tried to fill his shoes. But she shut me out and something inside her seemed to go cold."

As Katherine continued, he learned that Reece had been a normal child; she was a bit spoiled, but a very charitable and loving kid. Katherine looked away from him as she spoke. She focused on her cup, circling it with her finger and sipping it at times. She spoke of her daughter as if Reece were a puzzle of some kind and pieces of her were hidden deep inside the cup she held.

"Reecie became rebellious at fifteen," she continued. "As a high school teacher for many years, I was quite prepared for a headstrong daughter. But nothing prepared me for what happened in 1988." Katherine took a big sip of her tea and Steven sat eagerly listening.

"She talked me into letting her spend the weekend with this strange-looking girl who seemed fascinated with the color black. I mean, black fingernails, black lipstick, black hair and eyeshadow and clothes."

"Did Reece go black too?"

"No." Katherine lifted her cup and took another sip. "The girl's parents never seemed to be home. I don't remember the kid's name. I always called her the little girl in black." She went on to say that the girl-in-black gave a wild weekend party and some kid brought a Ouija board for entertainment. She swore that was when she lost her daughter. But she wasn't alone, she said. Other parents complained that their kids returned home visibly shaken and refused to speak about what went on at the party. A few kids had to have professional counseling, while others talked their parents into relocating. Katherine said Reece also refused to speak of that night and soon became hostile—even violent. Reece attacked her so viciously one night, she had to be hospitalized. Another time, she strangled Katherine and left her unconscious on the bathroom floor. A concerned neighbor found her hours later.

"I told the police it was an intruder who did it. I couldn't let them lock my baby away. You understand?"

"Of course."

"Anyway," she said, "stranger things began happening—some, not far from here." Katherine said that animals were found mutilated; family members disappeared; and a young girl was murdered…

nailed up-side-down to a tree. She was split up the middle, and her throat had been cut, almost to decapitation. During that time, Katherine said she and Reece fought constantly. Then she ran away.

"It was years before I knew where she was."

"And you think all of what you've told me had something to do with *this* Ouija board?"

"I'm sure of it." She bent forward and spoke as if she didn't want the walls to hear. "My daughter's soul is in that Ouija board." Then she sat back, looking strangely unconcerned, and sipped her tea.

Steven looked from under his lashes at Katherine. "You think the Ouija board took Reece's soul?"

"I don't think. I know. Haven't you been listening?"

"Yes." Steven didn't know what else to say. "Um." He pretended to care about the time. He quickly looked at his watch and stood. "Mrs. Dawson, thank you so much for talking with me."

Katherine walked him to the door. Of course he didn't believe one word of the story. He had no intentions of contacting her again since nothing she had said could be used to prove that her daughter was a phony. But he didn't believe she was, in any way, covering for Reece. She really believed some kids playing around with a Ouija board caused all those things that happened—if, indeed, they did happen. Steven figured her to be just one more poor fool caught up in the supernatural. He got into his rented car and headed to the airport.

Chapter Two

A MEETING OF THE MINDS

S teven parked his car fifty feet from Dr. Connelly's light brick mansion. He watched Reece Weatherbee and her chubby assistant, Debbie, step from a late model black Cadillac STS onto the narrow strip that led to Connelly's home. The walkway divided a large stretch of lawn covered with brown, yellow and burnt orange leaves; it reached from an iron gate to designer front steps. They stood before a carved mansion door with Old World glass and solid wrought iron grilles. An African-American woman opened the door. She smiled and motioned the women to come into the house.

Steven looked on curiously. For over a month, he had been faithfully following Madame Reece's every move. He longed to get into her house and snoop around, but never found it unoccupied. He learned that Reece was a creature of habit, but today she did something differently. And there it was. And who was this new person she was visiting? He tore open a large bag of Utz potato chips and began to munch. He kept his eyes on the front door.

Inside, Reece and Debbie sat quietly, their eyes taking in all the treasures of the room. On the wall was an early 1950s Jackson Pollock original abstract painting; under the painting sat two antique dark cherry accent chairs. Between the chairs stood a table that held a nineteenth century Chinese porcelain lamp. At the right of Reece, on a carved wood table, sat an odd-looking porcelain object that looked half dog–half lion. Reece moved closer to get a better look at the thing.

"Chinese Famille Verte Porcelain," Dr. Connelly spoke loudly from the doorway. "It's called a Foo Dog or Temple Lion."

Reece looked up at a tall, well-groomed, elderly man. Connelly walked towards her smiling, with both hands extended to her and Debbie.

"Oh, how interesting," Reece said and shook his hand. Debbie spoke, shook his hand and quietly went to the far side of the room so Reece and Connelly could talk privately.

Connelly went on to explain that the object of her interest was created around the early nineteenth century. It was known as a Buddhistic Lion. The Chinese believed it would guard against bad spirits and bring good luck. Nearly every household had one, he told her.

"Well, this whole room seems one big history lesson. I hope you don't mind my being so inquisitive."

"Not at all, Ms. Weatherbee."

"Please, call me Reece."

"Very well, Reece. Can I have Roberta get you and your assistant anything—tea, coffee, or something a wee stronger maybe?"

"No thank you. I really can't stay long. I'd like to make this as pleasant and as brief as possible."

"Very well," Connelly said.

He invited Reece to take a seat on the light blue sofa with large, checkered colored back pillows. He sat at the end of it and smiled.

"I'm really impressed with you," he said.

"Why is that?"

"Of all the letters I sent, you were the only spiritualist who was gracious enough to accept my invitation to discuss this most pressing matter."

"Your fine impression of me may not last."

"What do you mean?"

"I was asked to come and voice some concerns."

"Asked by whom?"

"My fellow psychics."

"But psychics are all over the world. Surely you don't represent them all."

"Only the ones affiliated with the PPS, our organization."

"And that stands for...."

"Paranormal Psychic Society–named by our late Madame Sonji Moals. She and twelve other psychics started its first coven back in the late nineteen eighties. We have over forty thousand members world-wide. Every five years, five hundred of our top officials meet right here in the states for a special celebration."

"That's very interesting; but why did you say I'd soon not be impressed with you?"

"We want you to stop writing about us."

"But that's what I do."

"Your writings make us out to be monsters...Boogie men hiding under kid's beds. You've called us everything from devil worshippers to even suggesting that we had something to do with the recent kidnappings and killings."

"But you did–in a way."

"You mean the portal we are allegedly using to summon demons through?" Reece paraphrased a line from one of Dr. Connelly's articles.

"That's exactly what I mean."

"What we do is bring the living and their dearly departed to-gether again."

"You know that's not true."

"You don't believe me?"

"I've studied psychics for years. I know what you're capable of."

"Please, I don't want to argue–just stop the writings."

"I can't. It's my civic duty."

"And is it your civic duty to incite people to boycott our businesses and conference meetings... to write graffiti on our homes and cars? They even threw a brick through one of our member's window during a séance. They could have killed someone."

"I apologize for the brick, but not for the truth I'm telling."

"Then you refuse?"

"You've opened a portal to a demonic world. That's not only evil, it's dangerous. What do you hope to gain by doing that? Do you have any idea what deadly consequences this can have on innocent living beings?"

"We bring the living and their dearly departed together again. That's all," she said sternly.

"That's not what you do and you know it."

"You are wrong about us."

Connelly's jaw tightened and he squinted as his eyes made contact with hers. "Reece, people are dying–many more are missing. Woman–you are playing with fire–Hellfire."

"How can I convince you that those mishaps had nothing to do with us?"

"I've seen your handiwork."

Reece's face grew into a frown. "What handiwork?"

"Twenty years ago–a demon stood before me and taunted me. I know how it got here. I know you psychics were behind it. Whether innocently or intentionally, you must convince your colleagues to stop this hideous practice."

"What if, for the sake of argument, you're right? No amount of writing can stop us."

"Then why are you and the PPS so worried about what I do?"

"Because it's a damn nuisance, that's why. And because some people are starting to believe it and taking their frustrations out on our property."

"I don't mean to cause you any inconvenience. But this portal that you've opened is far more dangerous to us all than what some people are doing to you and your members."

"Then you won't stop?"

"I can't."

Reece looked sternly at Dr. Connelly and sighed. "I was hoping we could settle this peacefully."

"Peacefully? As opposed to what?"

"I think you know," she said without blinking.

"Is that a threat?"

"No. Not from me. This is much bigger than just me."

"I see."

Reece stood up to leave. "Well, I did what I came to do. Too bad we couldn't come to an agreement."

He walked her and Debbie to the door. He stopped and placed his hand gently on Reece's shoulder.

"I *will* find a way to stop you," he said.

"Good luck," she said with a smirk. Then she turned and walked out the door with Debbie tagging behind like a well-trained dog.

Outside, Steven ripped off the wrapper of a candy bar and bit a chunk. He froze when he saw the women coming out the door. He watched as a tall, distinguished and slightly balding man stood in the doorway. The women got into the car and drove off. Steven snapped a picture of Connelly and memorized the address. He caught up to the black Cadillac as it veered off the quiet street and onto the hectic highway.

*****

One week later, Steven secured his own meeting with Dr. Connelly. He stood admiring the luxury items display. He recognized the famous 1952 Pollack painting, *Blue Poles*. It was his favorite. As he looked about, his eyes settled on the odd piece that had so fascinated Madame Reece.

"Chinese Famille Verte Porcelain," Dr. Connelly called from the doorway. "It's call…"

"A Buddhistic Lion," Steven said, interrupting him, "nineteenth century. Chinese believed it would ward off evil spirits and bring them good luck."

"Well, well, young man. I see there's a mutual interest here."

"Yes, sir."

"History major?" Dr. Connelly asked.

"Physics, sir."

Dr. Connelly held out his hand, and Steven shook it. He was delighted that he had impressed Dr. Connelly. With his sharing enough of Connelly's interest, he hoped to put the old man at ease; then he'd worm his way into finding out what went on between him and Madame Reece.

The men sat and talked about their interest in Chinese art and Jackson Pollock paintings. Afterwards, Steven felt comfortable enough to pop the question.

"It seems you and I may have something else in common."

"Oh?"

"What do you know about a Madame Reece…this psychic guru?"

"You know Madame Reece?"

"Not really. I went to one of her séances. I don't believe in that nonsense, but I attended to convince my friend that she was nothing more than a phony. But I failed." Steven went on to say that his friend was lining Reece's pockets with thousands of dollars, thinking she was putting her in contact with her dead relatives. He told of how his friend had turned her back on her religion and her family.

"It's like an addiction," he said. "I feel like my friend is drowning, and I don't have a rope to throw her."

"I detect your friend is more than just a friend?"

Steven, uneasy, ignored the question. "What do you know

about this woman, Doc?"

"What do you know about the supernatural?"

"I don't believe in it."

"Then I can't help you."

"What do you mean you can't help me?"

"Son, Madame Reece is not a phony. If you want to help this friend of yours, that's the one thing you must come to terms with."

"You don't really believe this woman talks to the dead."

"No. Once you die, you're gone. Nobody can conjure you up. Don't get me wrong, I do believe in heaven and hell. Nobody can bring you back but God."

"Now you've lost me. If the dead are gone and can't be brought back except by God, which I don't believe in either, then that makes her a phony–right?"

"Not entirely. She is a phony when she claims to talk to the dead. It's who she's really talking to that's so disturbing."

"Who?"

"Demons–not dead, yet not living. The reason people are fooled is that demons know everything about us. They hear everything we say and see everything we do. They can take any living form and look and sound like the people the living once knew. The one thing they can't do is hear our thoughts. Only God can do that."

Steven chuckled. "Doc, with all due respect, that's even crazier than Madame Reece. So let me get this straight: Madame Reece is not talking to dead people, but to demons that look and sound like the dead people she's supposed to be conjuring up."

"Exactly."

"Okay." Steven stroked his brow and tried to keep a straight face.

"You don't believe me."

"Doc, I'm sorry, but I think coming here was a waste of your time."

"You mean a waste of *your* time."

"All right, a waste for both of us."

"I don't care about your non-religious belief–that's your business. I just feel sorry for that friend of yours. Unless you believe what I've told you, you'll never be able to convince her."

"You're saying, unless I believe this entire religious jumble, I have to stand by and do nothing?"

"It isn't religious jumble. I saw a demon with my own eyes. It disappeared right in front of me. I lost my composure and had to keep myself from running from the platform where I was lecturing. I know you think people like me are delusional, but the spirit world is very real and sometimes very dangerous."

"But isn't God supposed to be a spirit?"

"I'm talking about the spirit world that Madame Reece and her kind deal in."

"I see." Steven could see disappointment on Dr. Connelly's face. He felt sorry for the old guy. He'd hoped that the Doctor could have shed more light on Reece so he could make a better case against her to Esther. But he now knew he'd have to do this on his own. Steven was about to thank him and leave when Connelly offered him a drink.

"Sure," he said.

Dr. Connelly walked over to a mirrored wall. He touched it, and a bar rolled into view.

"What's your pleasure?"

"A Captain Morgan would be nice, sir."

Connelly filled two glasses with ice and poured a shot of Golden Puerto Rican rum in each one; he filled both glasses with Coca-Cola and added a dash of lime. He walked back to the sofa, sat across from Steven and handed him the drink. Steven took a sip and listened as Connelly informed him further.

He talked of how long he'd been chasing these sorcerers and

the seriousness of Madame Reece's threat via the PPS. Steven had never heard of it; he questioned Dr. Connelly thoroughly and showed quite an interest in Connelly's meticulous research on the organization. Though nothing seemed to convince Steven of this pictured demonic world the Doctor tried to paint for him, he was, however, taken aback when Connelly mentioned the same dead girl that Katherine Dawson had mentioned to him weeks ago. The more Dr. Connelly talked, the more Steven realized how dangerous this was for Esther.

"Doc, I appreciate all that you've told me about Madame Reece and this PPS. But I'm afraid you and I are not on the same page with this. You seem to think that the only way to beat these people is to fight magic with magic, when clearly this is a matter for the police."

Steven finished his drink and stood up to leave.

"You're wrong, son. But I wish you all the luck with your friend. If you need me, I'm here." Dr. Connelly walked him to the door and ushered him off with a wave.

"Thanks for taking the time. I'll be in touch if I need any more information," Steven said from the walkway.

"Like I said, I'm here. And you take care," Dr. Connelly warned.

"I will," he said. He got into his car and drove off.

Chapter Three

THE FORCES OF EVIL

Steven pulled up to Madame Reece's home. It was an early 1920s red brick colonial house with white trimmed windows that sat far off the main street. A thick wooded area served as part of its oversized backyard. To its far left, a small brook glittered under a full moon. He shut the door of his Ford hybrid. The sound hovered over the silence as he stood checking out the areas that surrounded the house. Madame Reece had traveled with her entourage to Cleveland. Her closest neighbors were off to their summer homes. He had done his homework.

A cool wind whistled through the trees that towered over the house. Their long reaching branches seemed almost territorial as they slapped the top of the roof and beat senseless the red brick chimney. Steven walked the narrow path to the house; a chill gripped him. He tugged on the zipper of his short sports jacket that was midway and pulled it up to his neck. The closer he came to the house, the colder he became.

He twitched his nose; perhaps a dead animal in the woods, he thought. Suddenly his car keys felt like an ice cube in the palm of his hand. Halfway there, he was chilled to his bones. By the time he reached the side of the house, his teeth were chattering and water vapor fogged from his nose and mouth. None of this deterred Steven as his flashlight peered around for the opening. He had checked out the house when Reece had left for a couple of hours and knew there was a boarded-up window in the basement. He'd decided then, when he came back, this would be his entrance.

Once inside, he stumbled through the blackness with his flashlight and fumbled for his camera. The darkness was eerie and deathly silent. It yielded the kind of feeling you'd get if walk- ing alone at night in a graveyard. He bumped into many things he didn't recognize, and snapped with his camera everything that looked interesting or strange. And there were many. A few minutes into his snapping, the flashlight suddenly went out.

"Damn!" He clicked the switch and then banged the flashlight against his palm. But it seemed dead. "Shit!" He kept banging away at the thing, but nothing happened. "Christ!" Another bang and it burst on.

He pointed the flashlight and snapped the camera on a pile of books, a strange-looking calendar, and an open brown case with a medieval dagger. Steven kept snapping away until something caught his eye in a deep corner. There in the darkness, a pair of eyes glared at him. He gasped and broke for the window, dropping the light. He stopped short of scrambling for the opening, when he noticed the noise he made breaking for the window was the only sound. He listened but heard nothing coming after him. He saw the flashlight rolling in a half circle on the floor where he'd dropped it. He swallowed hard, took a few steps and picked it up. He kept the light beaming on the twin glares in the dark corner. With every step, his heart seemed to skip a beat. Slowly he inched towards them, closer and closer. He stood directly facing the eyes. But he deflated with a deep sigh and chuckled when he saw they were the glass eyes of a man-size stuffed animal.

Feeling relieved, he walked around freely after that, pointing and snapping. He pointed it up at the ceiling, then down to the concrete floor. On the concrete he saw a most unusual pattern. He couldn't quite make it out, but thought it looked like a huge Ouija board. He stepped back a few spaces and pulled the focus back on his camera and snapped. A sound, like a large stack of news-papers falling, came from behind. Steven whirled around and shined the light, but saw nothing. Again, the sound, but this time closer. He whirled around in the opposite direction, both hands on the flashlight like he was pointing a gun…his camera dangled from his wrist on a strap. But there was nothing there. A foul odor permeated the air; Steven sensed a presence coming up on him. He turned and scrambled for the boarded-up window but in his panic, he couldn't find it.

"Who's there?" he said, jerking around in every direction and pointing the flashlight like a crazy man.

The paper-crashing sound moved closer and louder towards him.

"I…I have a gun," he lied.

A freezing cold swept over him. He shivered and his teeth began to chatter. Stench like a rotting corpse hung in the air. He felt sick to his stomach. With his hands trembling, he pointed the flashlight in the direction of the crashing sound. There was nothing there but the foul odor. He lifted the flashlight higher and gasped when he saw the boarded up window on the other side of the basement. In his panic, he had scrambled in the wrong direction. Now this unknown thing stood between him and the outside world.

Steven shut off his flashlight and braced himself. Unable to see what was after him, he made a mad dash in the direction of the window. He swerved, stumbling blindly into everything in his path, thrashing about like some wild animal caught in a net. He reached the window and fumbled blindly for the right one with the loose boards that covered it. His hands burned from scraping along the brick wall; he ignored the pain and felt even harder for it. "Where is that damn window?" he blurted, searching blindly in the dark. He felt the sinister presence, a decaying breath on his head and neck. Terrified, he felt harder for the boards, his hands sticky with his own blood. He clawed at the brick wall for the window.

Finally, his fingers felt the boards and the outside cold. He pulled himself up, half out of the window, and breathed in freedom. But an icy grip took hold of his leg and snatched him back. The cold surrounded him and he went smashing to the floor. Something heavy leaped on him to force the life from him as he lay helplessly upon his back. He felt as if an elephant was crushing him. Steven tried to yell, but there was no breath. He thrashed his arms and kicked wildly, but was only slicing the air. He thrashed and kicked until he felt his eyes pop forward. Gasping his last bit of air, he thought the name of his love, though she would never know it. His thought was Esther. Lights burst inside his skull…and everything went black.

*****

Steven, in what seemed a fog, found he was on a dark road, running from the crashing sound with its decaying odor. He stopped running, turned and asked it, "What do you want?"

"A body," it said.

Steven pointed to a raven in flight and said, "Take him."

It snatched the raven out of the air and put it on like a coat.

"Are you satisfied?" Steven asked it.

"Yes, Mr. Crane, Mr. Crane, Mr. Crane."

Steven opened his eyes and found Madame Reece leaning over him, repeating his name. He lay in a large bed. His head and chest were bandaged. Debbie gave him a sip of brandy. Another assistant busied herself about the room.

Madame Reece stood over him, smiling. "You gave us quite a scare, Mr. Crane," she said.

"You remembered my name?"

"Of course."

"How long have I been here?"

"What were you doing in my basement?"

He put his hand to his head and stretched his eyes. "What the hell attacked me?"

"Nothing attacked you," she said, stone-faced.

"Oh, I suppose I did all of this to myself?" he said, touching his bandaged body and head.

"You have a slight concussion and a bruised chest. No bones are broken," Reece assured him.

"And you know this how? What did you do…conjure up some dead doctor from the other side?" He made light of her *so-called* psychic gift.

"We found you with a gash on your head and a very heavy file cabinet on you."

"Oh–so it was a file cabinet that attacked me?" He tried to lift himself, but felt dizzy and plopped back down on the bed.

"Now don't exert yourself," Debbie warned. She pressed another glass of brandy to his lips.

"You still haven't said what you were doing in my basement," Reece demanded.

He strained to sit up again; his head thumped as he stirred.

"First let me say, I appreciate your taking care of me like this. But you asked me a question so I'm going to answer you. I think you are a phony and a crook," he said. Reece raised an eyebrow.

"Now wait a minute," Debbie snapped. "Why…you ungrateful son of a bitch."

"Let him talk, Deb," Reece interrupted.

Steven went on to say how he felt about her getting her hooks into people with her phony psychic act. He mentioned, particularly, his friend (not calling her by name) and the money she spent on this farce of her talking to the dead. He said this obsession his friend had was ruining her life and her relationship with her family.

"And this person you're trying to help doesn't believe you?"

"No," he said, looking off.

"So what exactly did you hope to find digging around down there?"

"I don't know–something, anything that would have helped me prove you were a scam artist."

"Well, that's an improvement." Reece grinned. "I've gone from a phony and a crook to an *Artees,*" she joked, emphasizing the word artist. Debbie and the other assistant chuckled.

Steven frowned. "I don't think you're funny."

The corners of Debbie's mouth pointed downward. "You should be thanking Madame for not letting you bleed to death on the concrete floor," she said. "I wanted to call the cops–so they would haul your scrawny little ass off to jail, but she stopped me. Not only that but…"

Reece interrupted Debbie and ordered her and the other assistant to leave the room. Debbie glared at Steven before facing the doorway, and the other assistant turned up her nose as both left the room. Reece sat on the side of the bed. She had a sympathetic look in her eyes. "May I call you Steven?"

"Sure," he said, looking unconcerned.

"I don't know what you expected to find down there in the basement; had you come to me, I would have answered any questions you had. What do you need to know?"

"I want to know how you did it. I was right there in the room and couldn't detect one trick. You didn't fool me, but I've got to admit, you're really good. Too good."

"You mean the séance–no strings on flying objects or contraptions hidden under the table. Stuff like that?"

"Yeah. How did you do it?"

"Did it ever occur to you that I might be legit?"

"Never."

Reece smiled and held out her hands to him. She spoke softly, almost a whisper. "Give me your hands."

"What for?"

"Trust me," she said, her eyes unblinking.

Reluctantly, he placed his hands in her hands–and she gripped them. She reared her head back and began to hum. Steven noticed that although her speaking voice was higher, her hum was deep and gravelly. Her body slowly moved from side to side. Steven smirked and shook his head at her nonsense, but didn't remove his hands. She spoke in another language and moaned as her head slowly bobbed back and forth. The moaning turned into a chant. He chuckled and continued to shake his head at her. As Madame's behavior became stranger, he felt a bit dizzy, but figured it was the head injury. Then a light fog crept into the room. A mysterious cold gripped him, like it had while walking up to the house and again in the basement. Steven blinked to see more clearly. He smelled a pleasant odor, not like the odor that nearly sickened him in the basement. This one was sweet, like jasmine.

He felt something soft and cold move across his face and heard a child giggle. The voice seemed to come from under the bed. Creaking noises came from the closet area. He felt something tickle his ear. Reece stopped chanting and began to speak clearly. She envisioned a small boy–about ten, she said. "His hair is black–cut short. He has almond shaped, dark brown eyes. I can hear his mother crying. I receive that he likes apples on a stick… butterscotch. I see the letters S and R. He likes to dig for things," she said.

No way could she know about my childhood friend, Ricky Stewart. He was hit by a car when we were ten. Steven had always felt it was his fault for throwing the ball in the street. The two of them stole money from their parents and bought games and books that were too adult for them. They buried them in a secret place. After coming home from school, they would run off, dig them up and play with them. They called it their buried treasure. He sat stunned as Madame continued.

"I see a boy lying in the street; there's blood coming from his nose and mouth. I feel the name Ricky. Yes. Dear Ricky, knock twice little one, if it's you." One loud knock came from the closet area, then quickly another, more loudly.

Steven pulled his hands, but Reece held them tighter. "Stop this. I don't know how you know these things."

"Hush," she said. "He wants to speak to you." Reece's eyes began to roll and an eerie image, the likeness of Ricky, appeared in the light fog just above the bed. It giggled and greeted Steven in Ricky's voice. Steven's eyes grew wide and he jerked, but Reece held on to his hand, so as not to break the spell.

"Ask him anything," she said. "Quickly!"

Steven spoke just to play along. "Where did we bury our treasure?"

"By the old witch tree near...the school yard," it said. Once again he tried to pull away but her strength seemed inhuman as she held firm.

"Go on," Reece said, "ask him another."

His hands trembled like Esther's had at the séance. "Who bought them for us?"

"Drunken Mr. Kindle. Do anything for a cheap bottle of wine."

Steven was beside himself. His chest rose and fell rapidly as his heart thumped.

"How did we get the money?" But there was no answer. "Where did we get the money? Hello!"

"He's gone," Reece said.

"Gone. Gone where? Hey you!"

"It's no use; he's gone; but...wait! I'm getting a message."

"What message?"

"He says... he forgives you for throwing the ball in the street."

That's it, brother. Steven gasped and wrested his hands away from hers. "Damn you...you freak!" He kicked wildly at her; the covers flew in all directions. The bedside table overturned and a pitcher of water crashed to the floor.

Madame Reece let out a sound, like a mild roar. She collapsed, as she often did after contacting the other side. Her appearance was hideous. The women, hearing the commotion, came storming into the room. Steven was still shouting and kicking at her. After a few minutes, they convinced him to drink a brandy which, unknown to him, was laced with a sedative. When he had calmed, they collected Reece and took her from the room.

Steven floated through a fog, then found himself on the dark road: him, the raven and Ricky. Only the raven wasn't a bird anymore. They were arm in arm, skipping along and humming Madame Reece's moaning tune. He opened his eyes and found he was alone in the room. He struggled to get up but felt groggy; he seemed to move in slow motion. After his head cleared, he put on some clothes, grabbed his flashlight and camera, then headed for the hallway.

Unlike the basement, which was pitch black, a dim light lit the hallway. Steven roamed around trying to find something interesting to snap; when he felt something behind him, he put his flashlight in a defensive position and whirled around. Debbie stood with her hands on her fat hips.

He blew his breath hard. "Damn! You scared me."

"I'm not even going to ask," Debbie said. "Get back to your room. Madame don't like people roaming around at this hour."

"Why–afraid I'll find something?" he said sarcastically.

She wobbled back to her bedroom, turned and stood in the doorway. "Suit yourself, but I'd watch out for that file cabinet if I were you." She threw him a creepy smile and closed the door.

Steven flinched and thought he felt a cold finger on his neck. He took a quick glance over his shoulder, then up the dim hallway and back. Right out of the air, he heard the strange sound he'd heard in the basement; he scrambled back to the room and locked the door. After pushing a tall chest of drawers against the door, Steven took a gulp of brandy to relax. He polished off the bottle and slept through the night.

Days later, Steven felt well enough to leave. The house gave him the creeps. Plus, he couldn't shake the feeling that Reece was up to something. But because she was allowing him to leave, he felt, somehow, it wasn't about him. He excused himself from joining her at breakfast. Everyone acted as if the basement and the bedroom séance had never happened. Steven really didn't want to focus on it anyway. He had a million questions and no answers. He hadn't finished with Madame, but realized he was no match for her either. He needed a more sophisticated approach–though not the one Doc Connelly had talked about. He wasn't quite willing to believe all that stuff Doc had told him about demons and portals and the like, but he was convinced that there was something strange about Madame Reece--something that was outside of any reality he knew. And more than ever, he had to keep Esther away from her.

As he bade Reece and her staff goodbye, he never dreamed he'd be leaving her house by the front door. As he was fastening his seat belt, he looked over at the house; up on the second floor was a young girl peering through the window. She looked about sixteen or seventeen. She was dressed in a dingy, pink oversized sweater and a wool scarf wrapped much too tightly around her neck. Her stare was doll-like and blank. She never moved or blinked. Steven drove off.

On the way home, he called Dr. Connelly and told him everything that had happened.

"You damn fool, you could have been killed," Connelly said.

"Ok, you got that off your chest."

"This is serious. You get over here right now; we need to talk."

"Can't. I'm meeting Esther for dinner."

"This is important. Can't dinner wait?"

"Nope! I've made plans."

"All right, but don't mention anything about this to her."

"Are you crazy? You think I'm going to ruin a romantic evening with nonsensical ramblings about ghosts and demons?"

"All right, Son—well, think on this while you're chewing; that thing that attacked you in the basement and the young girl you saw in the upstairs window?"

"Yes?"

"They're one and the same. Enjoy your evening."

"What! Hello?"

Chapter Four

MEETING OF THE HEARTS

While staring into his bathroom mirror, Steven made a face like a blowfish and gently pulled the razor across his tan cheek. He repeated the routine several times before patting his face with a towel and splashing on Blue Seduction. In his bedroom, he whistled while strutting around in his briefs and pulled a suit from his wardrobe. He danced over to the bed with his suit in his arms like a partner and placed it there. He matched up a shirt and tie, a pair of socks, and examined his shoes for a perfect shine. After dressing, he studied himself in the mirror, and smoothed his hand over his short, brown, tightly curled hair. He grabbed his car keys and headed down to the garage. At the restaurant, he waited for Esther.

He had known Esther since he was seven and she was five. They had played together at school and in the churchyard. Since each was an only child, they often considered one another the brother and sister they never had. But by high school, between his raging hormones and her developing buxom body, those feelings had changed. At least for him.

Since eighth grade, he had loved Esther and felt very protective of her. Just a scrawny little kid at first, but by age fifteen, tall and slim, he had won several amateur Judo championships and defended her honor on more than one occasion. While other girls saw him as a brainy nerd, Esther found him fascinating and fun. She was the only one who could hold a candle to him intellectually. In their senior year, at different universities, both worked in their respective fields as interns with assured possibilities of being hired after graduation: Steven, as a nuclear engineer, worked chiefly in design engineering at a private research and development laboratory, while Esther, a CPA major, worked for a Forensic Accounting and Consulting Firm.

Steven looked at his watch; it wasn't like Esther to be late for anything. He had waited half an hour. He tried calling her and found that his phone was off.

Esther ran her fingers through her glossy, long, auburn hair. Standing in front of the mirror, she flashed her hazel eyes of approval at the outfit she had chosen for the night, then dabbed White Diamond on her neck and throat. She tried Steven's phone once more before heading out the door.

"God! Pick up, will you?" she said.

He clicked on his phone and saw that she had called.

Message one: *Hey Steve, tried to catch you. Sorry, I have to ask for a rain check. Something's come up. Give me a call ASAP. Ok Stevie? Bye.*

Message two: *Steve, call me.*

Message three: *Pick up the damn phone.*

Message four: *By now you know I'm not coming...so–talk to you later.*

"Shit!" Steven said. He spoke so loudly people seemed almost frozen as they stared at him. Walking to his car, he called Esther.

She answered. "Where've you been?"

He said, "What the hell was so important that you couldn't make dinner? I had reservations, you know."

"Sorry."

"Sorry doesn't cut it."

"Got to call you back. I'm pulling up," she said.

"Pulling up where? Where are you?"

"Steve, I swear I'll make it up to you. I told you something came up."

"What the hell came up? Why the mystery? Is it a guy?"

"No, it's not a guy," she sighed. "I'd tell you, but I know we'll argue."

"Tell me you're not at a séance."

Esther didn't respond.

"Damn it, Esther…"

"Stop making a big deal of this. I'll call you as soon as I'm home. And…"

"Whatever!" he said, hanging up on her. Then he called Dr. Connelly and left a message.

Heading over to Reece's house, he drove through stop signs, raced through caution lights, and crossed in and out of lanes. He pulled up in front of the house and found the house dark and gloomy, just as it had been the night he broke in. He thought it odd that there were no cars in the parking spaces. Before he could make any sense of it, his phone rang.

"Doc," he said, feeling relieved.

"I got your message," Connelly said.

"I'm here at Reece's and Esther's not here."

"Haven't you had enough of that demon trap?"

"Relax. I'm not going in this time. Besides, there's no one here. Why did she lie?"

"Maybe the séance is being held somewhere else tonight."

"Why change the location?"

"You broke into her place. Remember? These people are funny about invasion of their sacred places. Reece may feel your intrusion broke some magic circle or some spell."

"Esther could have told me she was going."

"She probably didn't want you to follow her. Look, there's nothing you can do about it. So, why not swing by here? There are some things I need to discuss with you."

"I hope it's not more of that demonic talk."

"After all you've experienced at that house, you're still in denial?"

"I'm sure there's a scientific explanation. I was probably hallucinating."

"And I guess it was your hallucination that nearly crushed you to death in the basement. Oh—wait, it was the filing cabinet that did that. Just get your ass over here."

"Calm down. I'm on my way."

When Steven arrived, Dr. Connelly had mixed some drinks and had two glasses on chill. He really didn't have anything new to discuss; he wanted to keep Steven's mind occupied and off worrying about Esther until he could make contact with her again. Connelly tried once more to convince him that what he encountered in the basement and the incident with Ricky were real, but Steven proved to be a hard nut to crack. Dr. Connelly called him hopeless. But he couldn't know that although Steven fought him on every case in point, he also fought constantly with his own intellect. While Steven's reasoning wouldn't allow him to wrap his brain around the supernatural, the hair rose on the back of his neck when he remembered that misty image with Ricky's voice speaking about things only the two of them knew.

Nearly two hours later, his phone rang. "Esther, thank goodness, where are you?"

"I'm home."

"You all right?"

"Yes. I'm sorry about tonight. We can go out tomorrow night if you want."

She sounded so sincere and so sweet. He never could stay angry with her for very long. He paused and then answered. "Meet you at six?"

"Ok."

"Goodnight," he said.

He clicked off, then looked at Connelly and smiled. With Esther tucked safely at home, he decided to cut his visit short. He got home around midnight and went straight to bed.

*****

Steven shifted his body beneath the covers. Esther let out a passionate moan as his hands caressed her soft skin. He placed a sweet kiss upon her neck Their bodies moved like the rhythm of the waves as the raven hovered above them. Its giant wings covered them like a six-foot shadow.

"Make him go away," Esther pleaded. Steven hit at the raven and his hand smashed against the corner of the night stand. The pain jolted Steven awake. He sprang up in bed, grabbed his hand that was throbbing and looked over at the clock. It was 4:00 in the morning; nearly 14 hours to go before his special evening with Esther. After massaging the pain out of his hand, he settled himself and fell back to sleep.

Later that evening, after work, he rushed home to shower and dress. Kofi's was Esther's favorite restaurant, and Steven waited eagerly for her to arrive. He took a table by the window overlooking the lake. He watched as her car pulled up and stopped. She gracefully stepped out as the valet held the door and took her keys. Her legs were long and smooth; she had slender feet with shiny white-tipped toenails that were beautifully showcased in peep, three-inch heels. She wore a little black dress that hugged her curvy hips and round buttocks. The heavy dress shawl that hung off her shoulders revealed her peek-a-boo breasts. Her silky brown hair flowed in soft waves that framed her brown face. She captivated Steven's attention as she seemed to float towards the table he'd reserved for them. Her bright smile lit up his world.

He rose and greeted her with a hug, then pulled out the chair for her and took his seat. They chitchatted for a while before ordering. Neither wanted to spoil the evening by speaking about the disagreement they had the previous night. After dinner, they took a walk around the lake. He struggled to get up enough nerve to tell her how he felt. Steven had hired a private tour boat. During the short ride, he turned to her. "I apologize for the way I reacted last night," he said.

"The apology is mine. I shouldn't have stood you up."

Steven took her hands, held them and looked deep into her eyes. Esther looked away from Steven as if she knew what was coming.

"You know how I feel about you," he said.

Esther didn't answer but looked up at him. He pulled her close to him and passionately kissed her, but she was like ice in his arms. Steven felt awkward and stepped back. She searched his face and saw love and hurt staring back at her. She let out a soft sigh as she struggled to choose her words carefully.

"Steve, you know I'm very fond of you. I've always thought of you as a dear friend, but I'm not ready to have the kind of relationship that you want."

"You mean, not with me."

She cocked her head to one side. "I'm sorry."

"It ... it's... ok." His face wrinkled and his eyes lost their earlier sparkle. She held on to his arm as he stood facing the water. He wanted the curling blue waves to scoop him up. He wanted the ocean to part like it had for Moses—to swallow him up like it had the Egyptian army.

They hardly spoke anymore during the short ride. Later, while walking back to their cars, he assured Esther that he was fine with her wanting only his friendship. But he was lying. He felt the painful sting of her rejection like a hard kick to his stomach. They embraced and promised always to be there for one another. Their cars passed going in opposite directions; Esther glanced over at him and smiled, but he looked straight ahead and drove out of her sight.

*****

For the next several days, Steven stayed planted in front of his computer researching information on Madame Reece. It was a sure way of keeping his mind off Esther. Every once and a while, the hurt resurfaced, and he became depressed. Yet, nothing would deter him from convincing her that Madame Reece was a crook— and a mysterious one, at that. He researched the PPS and found that though this organization was a threat, it was not as worldwide as Reece had claimed. There were only three chapters in the world; each chapter had several hundred covens: one chapter in the US, one in Haiti, and a third on the coast of West Africa.

Steven also researched the death of the young girl Dr. Connelly and Katherine Dawson had told him about. According to police reports, the young girl was a runaway and had been reported missing for several months before being found murdered. The report was exactly as Mrs. Dawson had said; she was hung upside-down, split up the middle and her throat cut. The report also stated that the girl appeared to have been a human sacrifice. The police suspected a dangerous cult had committed the crime. The report further stated that after the closed-casket funeral, to her parent's horror, her body was dug up and stolen. Her parents made a heart-wrenching plea for their daughter's return, but her body was never found.

Weeks after her parents' desperate plea, sightings of the girl were reported in the small town where she lived and died. Police, as well as the girl's parents, dismissed claims that these sightings were anything but bogus. But, insanity took the lead in the form of a blog which had a cult following. Wherever there were sightings of the girl, gruesome murders, dead animals and kidnappings followed—at which time the followers tweeted cheers. The police refused to believe that those crimes had any connection to the dead girl.

Steven called Dr. Connelly with his findings. He told the Doctor that he was going to the small town where the girl was murdered to see what he could further find out.

"You'll go over my dead body," Doctor Connelly blurted.

"Oh lighten up, Doc. Am I a grown man or what?"

"Son, you don't know what you're up against."

"I can handle myself."

"Right, like you did in Madame Reece's basement."

"I won't make *that* mistake again."

"No. Now you're making a dumber one."

"Okay, what would you suggest I do? They're getting together in this little town for some powwow in a couple of days."

"What kind of powwow? Speak English."

"Don't know—some kind of convention or something. I forgot to tell you that while I was recuperating from my injuries, I hacked into Debbie's computer and copied some interesting stuff."

"Like what?"

"Oh–names of PPS members, their phone numbers, addresses, emails, and other PPS activities. Do you know these people come from just about every walk of life there is? And I kept seeing some stuff about a glass cat eye. I saw that quite a lot."

Connelly was ecstatic. "Son, I could hug you. That glass cat eye is code for a portal they're using to summone those ghastly creatures we've encountered. I had a feeling where it could be, but thanks to you, now I'm sure."

"Really? Then that's all the more reason we should go there. Don't you think?"

"No, no, no. I insist we don't go there just yet. There's more we need to know before we can make a move."

"But Esther is still fooling around with these people. I've got to know what they're up to."

"I understand your concerns, but it's too dangerous right now."

Just then Dr. Connelly's doorbell rang. "Steve, I've got to go—company's here. Now we're straight on you not going off by yourself?"

Steven sighed. "Yeah, we're straight."

"You don't sound convincing."

"Doc! I get it!"

"All right, keep digging. And I'll try to check back with you a little later–if not tonight, tomorrow."

"Tomorrow would be better."

"Okay, tomorrow then," Dr. Connelly said.

An hour later, Steven's laptop was still warm when he packed it and grabbed a cab to the airport for his flight to Cleveland.

Chapter Five

THE CHALLENGE OF GOOD AND EVIL

D istant voices woke her. The talking sounded muffled; it trailed off into silence. Esther whimpered and tried to raise herself, but discovered that she was bound. Her wrists were tied behind her back, and her knees were bent with a rope around her ankles that connected to the one on her wrists. The rope cut into her flesh when she strained against it.

Forcing her eyelids open, Esther battled to recover from the drug they'd given her. She blinked to adjust her eyes to the darkness that settled all around her like a heavy blanket. No one bothered to gag her. She was held so far from help that if she had let out an ear-piercing scream, no one would have come. For no one would have heard her. Not ever her captors. Staring into the blackness, she repeated aloud her favorite scripture for times of peril. "God is my refuge and strength, a very present help in times of trouble." After the words, her fear ceased, but the tears flowed. Esther forced against the rope again; it gave a little, but cut deeper into her flesh. She inched around in her confinement. Her prison was a small room, the size of a tall walk-in closet. She lay there repeating the scripture as hot tears streamed down and warmed her face.

Steven settled into his hotel room but felt too exhausted to unpack. He called Esther again and left a message, hoping she would get back to him. He hadn't heard from her in a couple of days. The flight to Cleveland had been marred by the heavy rain and fog which caused major inconveniences among travelers, leaving many stranded in its wake. Several main roads leading to the hotel where Steven stayed were blocked by floods or landslides, and some bridges were damaged and impassable. His cab ride along a graveled back road was long and bumpy.

Dr. Connelly had called several times and left messages, but Steven knew by now the doctor realized he had not kept his promise. Steven thought the last thing he needed was a fatherly lecture. He figured that once he was able to find out more about this organization, Doc would be so happy he'd forget about being angry with him.

He called room service and ordered dinner. Then he got on his laptop and spent an hour searching for more information on the PPS convention that was being held there. A knock came on the door. He spun around from his laptop, stood and fumbled in his pockets for a tip while walking to the door. He opened it and Connelly stood grinning with his laptop and a stack of notebooks in his arms. The two men stood silent for a moment.

"So I lied. How did you know I was here?" Steven asked.

"When was the last time you did what I said?"

"Yeah, but how did you know it was this hotel?"

"You don't hide very well. Are you going to ask me in or what?"

Steven smirked and walked away, leaving Dr. Connelly only a foot with which to close the door behind him. The men had exchanged a few sharp words when Steven's phone rang.

"Hello," Steven said, still in his sharp voice.

Connelly looked for a place to unload the pile of notebooks and heard Steven apologize for his sharp tone. Then he noticed a troubled look slowly growing on Steven's face. He set the pile on the table and eased down in a chair. He seemed to understand the call from the one-way conversation. Mid-way through it, Steven's eyes appeared watery. It was Esther's father—she was missing. The Reverend and Mrs. West became frantic when the FBI tracked her phone signals across state lines.

After the call, Steven seemed in slow motion, as he placed the phone on the table. He put both palms to his head and plopped down on the sofa. Connelly poured a glass of water and handed it to him, which he ignored. He sat doll-eyed and stared at nothing. After a long moment, he broke the silence.

"I've got to find her," he said, his mouth drooped.

"I have a feeling if we find the PPS, we'll find Esther," Connelly said.

"You think Reece is behind this?"

"This is what she does."

"If that bitch has laid one finger on her…I swear …I'll…"

"Calm down. That was smart of you not to mention to her parents what we know about Madame Reece. This may surprise you, but many Christians find it hard to believe this kind of evil exists outside of the Bible."

"What was I supposed to say? And why are we just sitting here? We should be phoning the police."

"And tell them what–that she's being held captive by a sorcerer who talks to demons? And how long do you think it will take them to order us matching straitjackets?"

"So what then? I'm losing it just sitting here doing nothing; what she must be going through…all alone…and…"

"We don't know how many there are. That's why we have to wait and think this thing through."

"Think… there's nothing to think. I'm going after her." Steven got up to grab his jacket.

Connelly grabbed his arm. "When are you going to realize that this is about more than just Esther? Everyone who comes in contact with these people is in danger."

"I don't care about anyone else."

"But don't you see? If we move too fast, it might scare them off. And we may never find them again. They are notorious for disguising themselves and keeping a low profile for years."

"I'm not listening to this; I'm on the next flight out of here."

Dr. Connelly jerked Steven back and glared at him. Steven had never seen such a look on Connelly's face before. Dr. Connelly's lips tightened. "Now you listen to me. I've researched and tracked hundreds of cults for over twenty years. I'm this close," Connelly held up his thumb and forefinger showing an inch between them, "from stopping one of the deadliest groups of people on this planet, and if you think I'm going to allow your lovesick ass, over a woman who doesn't even want you, screw things up...you're sadly mistaken!"

At that moment, the blood drained from Steven's face. *I can't believe he just said that.* Steven turned–walked over to the window, shoved both hands in his pockets and gazed out. *I confided in him like he was my own father, and he just throw it back in my face like this?*

Connelly stood awkwardly–shifting slightly from foot-to-foot and not knowing what to do with his hands. "Son, I didn't mean to go there."

"Just leave."

"Steve..."

"Leave."

Connelly gathered up the things he had brought and walked to the door. He opened it and glanced over his shoulder at him; Steven appeared so fragile. Connelly slowly closed the door behind him. Steven just stood and stared out at the storm.

*****

It was beginning to get light. Esther noticed the window above her. A twelve-foot ladder was needed to reach it. The light streamed through. It bounced off the solid walls of her confinement and fell over her handbag that had been tossed in with her. The contents had spilled out and were scattered about the floor. She could see her compact, wallet, keys and cell phone. She rolled over to maneuver her fingers to grab the compact. Her wrists burned and bled. She wiggled, squirmed and stretched as her fingers inched toward it. Her hands were bound so closely to her body that she couldn't get a good reach.

She rested for a while, then strained against the ropes again. It was minutes before she reached it; when she did grasp the compact, it slipped from her bloody fingers. After so much straining, her hands began to cramp and became painful balls. Esther moaned and tried to straighten her hands but couldn't. Rocking in pain, she lay there until the blood dried, then gripped the compact and held it tightly. She struck it against the floor. The broken edge gnawed away the rope from her hands. After cutting the rest of her body free, she grabbed the phone, but found that the batteries had been removed. She flopped against the wall, letting the phone slip from her hand, and sobbed.

*****

Steven juggled eating and keying on his laptop. He felt disappointed that he couldn't leave and find out what had happened to Esther. He was stuck there while city workers struggled to clear main roads and bridges. The heavy rain had caused the cancellation of all flights leaving Cleveland. After hours of staring at his laptop, his eyes grew tired and he felt exhausted; he settled back on the sofa and took a snooze.

Dr. Connelly busied himself with learning the exact location of the PPS convention. He didn't believe it was an actual convention, but a code word in emails for a special gathering they were having. Dr. Connelly knew these gatherings were always about some sinister practice. He learned they had leased an old mansion on Kingston Hill, about three miles outside of Ohio. The mansion, built in the early 1800s, was set high on a hill. It had stood unoccupied for several years until purchased in 1898 by a wealthy middle-aged gentleman named Henry Frederick De Hunskull. No one ever knew why, after a short time living there, he murdered his beautiful young wife and drowned their seven–year-old twin daughters. Some say he went mad because the mansion was haunted. It seemed something similar had happened there ten years earlier. When the police arrived, they found that Mr. De Hunskull had gouged out his eyes and hanged himself. Weeks later, the family dog was spotted in the front yard–dead with a human eyeball just inches from its mouth.

The room phone rang. Steven rose and clicked on the lamp next to the sofa where he lay.

"Hello," he said.

"Steve, now don't hang up. I just want to know if you'd heard anything about Esther."

"No." Steven clicked off while Connelly's voice still hung in the air.

He stretched and looked at his watch. He had been asleep for a couple of hours. He checked his phone and saw a strange number and clicked the message. When he heard Esther's frantic voice, he jumped straight up and dialed back. But he got nothing but static. For the next hour, he sat staring at his phone, willing it to ring. He paced back and forth, scratching his head. He wanted to call Dr. Connelly, but he wasn't speaking to him. After what seemed like an hour, the phone rang. Steven clicked the green button so hard, the phone nearly popped out of his hand.

"Hello!"

"Steve," Esther whispered.

"Baby. Oh God–where are you? Are you all right?"

"I'm in this huge house, like a castle."

"Castle...where?" He began to pace the floor.

"I think I'm still in Cleveland, though I'm not sure. I came with Madame Reece."

"Cleveland? That's where I am. What the hell are you doing here?"

"What are *you* doing here...how did you know I was here?"

"I didn't. I came here to check on Reece and this convention they're holding here. Then your dad called and said you were missing."

"I don't have time to explain everything. Just come and get me."

"Honey, of course, but where are you?"

"I'm not sure."

He stopped pacing. "Are you hurt?"

"Oh Steve, I should have listened to you. They all seemed so nice at first. We had a fine dinner, but after a few sips of wine, I suddenly felt dizzy. I complained, but they just looked at me, smiling–Madame too. The next thing I knew, I woke up all tied up in this small room with a high ceiling. But I got loose."

"That bitch!"

"I'm using a phone in the library, it's ...."

"You keep saying they...who else besides Reece? Esther? Esther! Damn!"

A knock came on the door. Steven hurried to the door and opened it. Dr. Connelly pushed by him.

"I have something to tell you," Connelly said excitedly.

"Whatever it is, it has to wait. I just heard from Esther. Reece didn't kidnap her, but she's holding her captive in some mansion here. Somehow Esther got away. But before she could tell me where she was, the phone went dead."

"Went dead, or did someone apprehend her?"

"I don't know."

"Then she must be there."

"There, where?"

"That's what I came to tell you. Madame and about two hundred of her followers are holed up at Kingston Hill in this huge nineteenth century mansion–some call a castle. They meet there once every five years for their most holy holiday where they make a human sacrifice to their demon god."

"Human sacrifice! No, God no–not Esther."

"That's why I rushed here. I have a plan."

"Great! What is it?"

"Now, remember what I said; this can't just be about Esther. If we go in…we go in all the way. I'm not leaving until I bring that place down around them," Connelly said sternly.

"I understand. Just tell me what to do."

"Can you drive in this weather?"

"Sure I can." Steven saw Dr. Connelly gripping a strange leather bag he'd never seen in his possession before. "Doc…what's that you're carrying?"

"It's everything I'll need to defeat Reece and her followers."

"But you're just *you*. Didn't you say these people were witches and that they dealt with demons and other dead stuff?"

"I didn't want to tell you this, because I know you don't believe in such things. But when I became aware of this evil twenty years ago, I began studying the Mystic Arts. While I don't mean to brag, I've become quite a master of it."

"Doc, you some kind of male witch?"

"I don't call myself anything. What I practice, I use for good, not evil the way they do. I'd appreciate it if you'd keep my little secret."

"Sure…but what's my part in all of this? I don't know any Voodoo."

"It's not Voo…never mind, I'll explain on the way." The men grabbed coats and umbrellas and made their way to a rented car.

Chapter Six

HELL BREAKS LOOSE ON KINGSTON HILL

Steven drove the Hummer like a madman through the suicide passage. The back road was treacherous, but it was the only road that led to the Kingston Hill mansion that wasn't washed out.

"Slow down, you fool; you'll get us both killed."

"You just sit back, old man, I got this."

Moonlight paled in comparison to the lightning flashes that surrounded the vehicle every minute like new suns bursting into flames. While wheel-high mud puddles swallowed up the path, Steven battled to compete with the high winds and treacherous rainfall. The car swayed against the bone-chilling winds as he pushed the engine towards the mansion. The one-hour drive that should have ended minutes before was still thirty minutes away, thanks to the menacing storm. The windshield wipers failed to smack away the rain as it fell too quickly against the glass. After over an hour's drive, Steven still struggled to see the road. Then as the headlights beamed, the dark mansion suddenly appeared like a black Hell made of stone, sitting high beneath a thousand tiny streams of pouring rain and a cracked sky of flashing bolts.

*****

Recaptured, Esther's naked body shivered from the cold. The inhabitants of the house went about their routine, deaf to her pleading until an attendant came to offer her comfort and to tell her how fortunate she was to be used for the *sacrifice*. She helped Esther with a small cup of strong tea, one sip at a time. The hot liquid revived her, and she began to beg for her life. The attendant looked no older than her and wore a black cloak with a hood that half covered her strawberry blonde hair. She stroked Esther's dark locks with her pale hand. Her eyes shone a strange mixture of sympathy and sinister mischief as she stared down at her victim.

But Esther seized the moment. She sprang from the cot like a pissed-off cat and wrestled the young woman to the floor. The two rolled about on the cold concrete with dark brown and blonde hair flipping to and fro and fists flying. After the women equally exchanged blows, Esther managed to get on top and pounded the woman in the face until she was unconscious. She rose and kicked her over with her foot, took off her cloak and covered herself with it. She tiptoed to the door, pressed her ear against it and listened. She slowly and carefully cracked it to peek out. Suddenly the door flew open, almost knocking Esther down; in seconds, several cloaked women were all over her. One of the women cried out when Esther's fingernails deeply raked across her face. Esther pulled chunks of hair from every head that got near her. She kicked and clawed her way to the open door like a madwoman. Not able to shake off the effects of the spiked tea, Esther saw double as she stumbled halfway down the hallway. When the women caught up and grabbed her, her protest became slurred and her resistance weak as she went limp in their grasp.

Meanwhile, the thunder bellowed outside the mansion as the heavy rain splashed against its morbid stone.

"Doc, I found a way in," Steven shouted. He smashed a large rock against the basement window.

"You know, you're starting to get good at this breaking and entering," Dr. Connelly joked.

Steven smiled as he led the way into the mansion. They walked in, but stopped midway and looked around the eerie quietness of the place. It looked like a huge warehouse nearly a block long and had a ceiling so high, it needed a fire engine ladder to touch it. On the ceiling, walls and floors were ancient markings of gothic themes, including a three-headed dragon, skeletons with swords, and horrified children's faces burning in flames.

"This looks identical to Madame Reece's basement, except larger. Everything is set up the same–the floor, the walls, even that stuffed animal there in the corner. I wonder what it means," Steven said. His mouth went dry and chills rippled up his back at seeing the exact scene where he'd almost died.

Connelly noticed some of the supplies that lined the shelves: chalices, Tarot cards, odd tea boxes, daggers, beeswax, candles, pendulums, oils, incense, herbal smokes, Native American smoke pipes—things that were well-known to him. Dr. Connelly wanted to explore more shelves, but the huge Ouija board design that covered a large area of the center of the floor captured his attention. He examined the heart-shaped hunk of wood, known as the planchette, used to communicate with demons. Dr. Connelly's face turned ashen as he encountered chilling vibes from the Ouija board.

Steven looked at Dr. Connelly and frowned. "You all right?"

"We've got to get out of here and find another entrance," Connelly said while slowly backing up.

Steven never asked him why, but he knew anything that made Connelly back up was not something he wanted to encounter. Steven quickly followed him out of the window and back into the clutches of the terrible storm. They scrambled through the rain until they found a stone staircase leading into another level of the mansion. Steven forced his way into, what seemed like, a large library. He checked the room, looking behind each door. One door led to a long hallway, and he cautiously cracked the door and peeked out. Then he signaled to Dr. Connelly that all was clear. Connelly breathed a sigh of relief.

"What happened to you down there?" Steven asked. "Wherever there's an active Ouija board, there's a portal opening."

"You mean where the supernatural can get through?"

"Precisely," he answered. "You see, demons are very territorial. Once they're permitted to come into our realm, meaning our world, they assign themselves to the very object used to bring them here. In this case, it is the Ouija board. But the board is not possessed. Demons can only possess living flesh unless that flesh was a sacrifice for their entrance."

Steven snapped his fingers. "Hey, the dead girl."

"Exactly," Connelly answered. "The only way to break their connection to this object is by using magic to send them back to their realm and sealing up the portal. Because they fear this, they will launch a deadly attack on any stranger who comes near the object. And they will kill even the ones who brought them here, if they suspect betrayal."

"So that's why it attacked me in Madame's basement. It thought I was there to destroy the Ouija board." Dr. Connelly nodded in agreement.

"Doc, since we now know this stuff, shouldn't we find Esther and beat the hell out of here?"

"Yes. But *you* find Esther. I've got to go back down. I've got to close that portal."

"But why split up? Can't we do both together?"

Dr. Connelly didn't answer, but pulled out the blueprints and floor plans of the mansion. He got down on his knees and spread the large sheets over the floor, smoothing out the wrinkles with his hand. Steven knelt down beside him.

"Now here is the main entrance of the mansion," Connelly began. "There are twenty-four rooms. You only have three hours to find which one Esther is being held in. She's not in danger yet, because these people are very meticulous about preparations and rituals and such. And of course, it's not midnight yet either. They do practically everything at midnight. Remember—only three hours to find her and get out."

"And you're staying here to do what?" Steven asked sarcastically.

"Son, you know what I must do. What I've always said I would do. These people have to be stopped."

Steven stood up. "You think I'm going to let you go down there alone?"

"I've studied and trained years for this. You've done all that I've asked you to do. Only I can do the rest."

"But you've been on my back from day one about me only thinking about Esther; now I want to help you take these people down, and you're telling me to go save her."

"If it weren't for your concern for Esther, you would have never sought me out. You almost got yourself killed finding out things I needed to know. It would have taken me additional years to find these people on my own. You go and find that woman you love and get her away from here; let me do what I've been ordained to do."

For the first time, Steven realized his deep feelings for the man. He felt both sad and proud at his willingness to put his life on the line. He headed for the door, then looked back at Dr. Connelly and spoke to him, he thought, maybe for the last time.

"I'm not hopeless, Doc." Steven said in a low voice.

Connelly pressed his lips together and nodded. Steven cracked the door, peeked out, and eased out of the room.

Chapter Seven

THE EYE OF THE WITCH

Steven's watch showed almost two hours to midnight. His search for Esther now placed him on the third level. He sneaked around, ducking in and out of shadows and was nearly spotted on several occasions. The love he felt for her mingled with hatred he held for her captors. The floor plans Dr. Connelly had given him seemed a godsend as he found that he stood within a few feet of one of few remaining rooms. As Steven turned the corner, he quietly darted back; a guard placed in front of a room meant only one thing—Esther. The guard's black, hooded cloak didn't hide his tall, muscular frame. His stern facial expression glowed with duty and honor like a Marine eager to lay down his life for his country. Steven knew getting past him wouldn't be easy.

He hid back against the wall, knowing full well that his actions would mean life or death for his beloved. Surprisingly, he recalled one of Pastor West's boring prayers. He allowed the words to echo through his mind, and they lit a fire deep within him like nothing had ever done before. He braced himself and took several deep breaths. Then like a flicker of lightning, he turned the corner and bolted towards the guard. The man barely had time to brace himself when Steven crashed into his chest, knocking him to the floor. Steven adjusted his body to execute a headscissor leg lock, but was shocked at how quickly the big man scrambled to his feet.

He hopped to his feet also. Both eased in close and assumed a defensive stance; they moved in a circular motion like wrestlers in a ring. The man punched Steven in the face so hard, he bounced off the hall wall. The man quickly followed with a left jab that caught Steven on the chin, reeling him to the floor; he stumbled to his feet, his eyes still a little blurry, and he shook his head.

Steven resumed his position and saw a right cross that swished past his right ear. Steven struck back with a crippling kick to the knee that bent the man down to his eye level, enabling Steven to do a leaping headbutt. While the man wobbled in a daze, Steven rushed behind him and locked him in a stranglehold, pulling him down to the floor.

Like a bull, the man tried to buck Steven off him. Several times, he nearly lost his grip on the man, but managed to hang on. At one point, the man struggled to his feet. Steven hung on, with his feet dangling off the floor. He tried to throw Steven over his head, but Steven tightened his grip and pulled the man back down. The man deliberately fell back on him, letting his full weight pin Steven to the floor, crushing him. Steven panted rapidly, his veins burst forth in his neck, and sweat poured down his face as he ignored the crushing pain and squeezed the man's throat. The man, gasping for breath, clawed viciously at Steven's arm, ripping pieces of his leather jacket sleeve. But Steven's arm was like a clinging python.

Finally, the bulging muscles grew still and the body went limp. Steven shoved the unconscious man off of him, fell back against the wall and gasped for air. Hoping no one heard the commotion, he looked up and down the hallway before getting up and entering the room. Turning the rusty doorknob, he pushed the door open and eased through. The room was empty except for a cot; it had no windows, and the room bore a heavy chill. Esther, naked and hiding under the cot, not knowing what was happening outside the door, looked up at him with glassy doe-eyes and a faint smile.

"Steve," she said in a hoarse voice.

"I'm here, Baby."

He signaled for her to stay put while he went back to the door to peek out; when he saw it was clear, he carefully, as not to revive the big guy, eased off his opened cloak. He walked back and kept his eyes away from her nakedness, holding the cloak in front of him as she rose from the floor. He wrapped it around her, and held her while she shivered from the cold.

Esther noticed a raised bruise above his right eye; her soft hand gently turned his cut chin towards her.

"Oh God…you're hurt."

"Don't worry, Honey, the other guy isn't doing too well either."

"I'm so glad you're here. I was scared. I didn't think you'd find me."

"Doc is here too, but he won't let me help him close the portal. He wants me to get you out of here. I know you don't know what's going on, and there's no time to explain."

"No, I do know. The man who was guarding me told me who Madame Reece really is and why she wants me. Something about a sacrifice."

Steven's bright face went dark. "Nobody's going to lay a hand on you."

"They also know you and Doc are here and what Doc is up to."

"They know?"

"Yeah. Madame laughed and said you'd come for me. She said Doc is a fool; he'll never defeat Lima. That's what she called it."

"Lima? That must be that thing that attacked me in the basement."

"Someone attacked you? What basement?"

"Honey, there's no time to explain."

Esther appeared nervous. She looked over at the door. "Oh Steve, can we just go?"

"Don't worry. I'll get you out of here. Doc is supposed to be some kind of wizard, and he's going to bring this place down."

"Doc, a wizard?"

Just as they made a move towards the door, it flew open. There stood Madame Reece, dressed ceremoniously, with six of her cloaked goons behind her, including the big guy who was still nursing his torn knee and sore neck. He looked at Steven with murderous eyes.

"Oh shit," Steven said under his breath.

Two goons rushed in, grabbed a handful of Steven's jacket in the back of his neck and jerked him out of the room and down the hall. Esther, Madame and the others closely followed, with the big guy limping behind.

*****

It was ninety minutes to midnight. The room bore all the signs of an interrogation chamber–empty but for chairs that were scattered about. Several tall, muscular men stood against one wall with their arms folded across their chests like seven-foot genies freshly released from their magic lamps.

Madame Reece sashayed back and forth; her full length hooded robe trailed behind her like the black train of a gothic queen. Her robe was the blackest of velvet: on the front were displayed seven red rose Chinese frog closures and button knots; the back of it bore the image of Tiamat...the Dragon Goddess of Primal Chaos. She clapped her hands once loudly; two of her goons brought Steven in, disheveled and bruised. They threw him at her feet and stepped back. Esther, who was tied to one of the chairs, could only look on with sad eyes.

"Mr. Crane," Madame spoke sarcastically, "it seems we're always meeting under the most fortuitous circumstances."

Steven looked up, his black stare fixed on her pale, cold face as she spoke.

"Maybe not so fortuitous, though," she teased, "since we all knew you'd come and try to save your precious little cunt here."

She threw Esther a cold stare. Esther raised her chin in defiance and stared back at her.

"What the hell do you want with us?" Steven blurted.

Straight away, a black boot blindsided him on the left side of his face.

"Quiet, you bastard! Speak only when you're told!" his attacker warned.

Steven cringed, doubled over and moaned.

"You leave him alone. I'm the one you want." Esther's said.

"Shut your mouth, Cunt!" yelled another henchman.

"No. Let Mr. Crane speak. Perhaps it is time he and his darling little Esther know exactly what we're doing here," Reece said menacingly.

The men all smirked and glanced approvingly at each other. Steven didn't like the sound of that.

"But if you tell me, you'll have to kill me, right?" he asked, knowing the answer.

"Obviously, but not right away," Madame joked.

The men chuckled.

"Then I pass," Steven said. His breath seeped out of him like his whole body was deflating.

"But Mr. Crane, you've come so far, breaking into my basement not once, but twice. Wouldn't you like to know what all your hard work was for? It's the least I can do before your untimely demise. Don't you think?"

His swollen lips leaked blood as he spoke. "All right. I deserve it. But not Esther. Let her go. Please."

"Let her go? Let her go? You idiot. You really don't know what you've stumbled into, do you?"

"I know all right. You're going to sacrifice her to some stupid thing you call a demon. Reece that's murder; you can't do it."

"Oh, but I can, and I will. Her blood will provide me with the power I've craved for twenty years. Power to rule over millions, to be the most powerful witch on this planet. And the great Lord Azi Dahaka will reward me tonight."

"What the hell is that?"

One of the men bent over him. "Not *That...Who*," he said.

Steven prepared himself for a hit, but was relieved when it didn't come.

"He is the Great Lord of witchcraft and a high demon with unimaginable power," Reece said, looking at Steven. "We worship him as the great spirit of vengeance." Approval and smiles rose on the men's faces. "Only a high-ranking witch, like me, is even allowed to summon him." She swirled around, her long train sweeping the floor, her eyes looking distant. She now spoke majestically as the men looked upon their dark queen. "When he comes through the Great Eye tonight, he will reward me with magic so superior that the universe will be mine for the taking. Under my rule, the earth shall be my footstool, and all flesh shall tremble at my feet."

"You're insane, you stupid degenerate." Steven chuckled from a stone-cold face.

A fist smashed against his right jaw. He heard the bone crack as a light flashed inside his head. Madame Reece watched as the blood trickled out of his nose and mouth. Dazed, he bent over; slowly he gathered strength and raised his head. He slurred his words as he pleaded, "Please, take me. Use me for your demon."

Esther's eyes filled as she watched Steven plead on his knees for her life. Madame Reece stepped forward and looked down upon him, flashing a sinister smile. "How noble you are, my dear," she said, stroking his hair, "but I'm afraid *your* blood won't do."

As she spoke, a chill crept through his body at the sight of her. Her face appeared off-white. Her dark eyes bore the glitter of a serpent. And looking up between her lips, Steven could swear he saw long pointed fangs. He dropped his head, stared down at the floor and thought. *Whatever Doc is planning, he'd better do it—and fast.*

Chapter Eight

STAYING ALIVE

It had grown dark in the room. Only the thinly scattered waves of light from Dr. Connelly's enchanted candle burned. His incantation produced a soft, crystal-like substance that reflected off the ceiling and formed an invisible shield around him–a ten-foot diameter globe that moved when he moved. This magical armor, tough like dragon scales, would prove crucial in warding off explosive attacks from a long distance. To prevent invisible assaults, Connelly would conjure *Darkness Walls* that could absorb energies of ghostly entities and turn their energies into optical light, making them tangible targets.

Lima, an awesome demon, would prove a most deadly opponent; summoned to earth's realm from Tartarus, an abyss of torture, it roamed as a lesser demon from a minor legion that patrolled the River Styx. Its powerful breath weapon projected electricity that could destroy flesh and bone in seconds. In close combat, it possessed poison abilities, including two-inch fangs and retractable claws. Its venomous spit could dissolve the hardest metals. No magic could destroy it. To defeat Lima, Connelly needed only to stay alive and use a spell to force it from the realm and then seal the portal behind it.

Dr. Connelly collected his enchanted weapons, including two powerful Talismans: a Tomb Ring and the *Eye of the Cock* crystal. *The Eye of the Cock* was a symbol of Christ's resurrection; it was said that ancient soldiers carried the *Eye* into battle and fought with overpowering strength because they believed they could not die. Connelly slid the Tomb Ring on his pointing finger, placed the weapons in a leather bag and fastened it to the green robe cord around his waist.

If he failed to defeat Lima, who protected the portal, Azi Dahaka would enter through—a nine-foot, dark scaly-skinned creature with two fanged cobras springing from his shoulders, complete with a halo of eyes surrounding his horned head. A Lord from his own realm, he would come with an entourage of spirits to attend his supernatural needs. His earthly appetite for blood would be insatiable: eating the equivalent of five live cows a day and requiring numerous human sacrifices. No mortal could control him. No magic could banish him. Once he entered a realm, he stayed and ruled.

Dr. Connelly concluded his meditation; he kissed the wooden cross that lay against his pounding chest and began the short journey back to the lower level of the mansion. He slowly, methodically descended the stairway, his long golden robe with blue trim quietly clearing each stone step behind him. Connelly faced the large wooded door at the end of the short hallway and opened it. He stood majestically, unblinking, unwavering and stared into the darkness.

There in the eerie silence, Lima, unseen by the human eye, guarded the sacred portal. Connelly moved slowly to the center of the underground level; he stopped a few feet short and just outside of the large Ouija board ornament on the floor. *The Eye of the Cock* rested snugly in the palm of his left hand. The dark held a deathly chill, and he appeared aware of the demon's presence. Standing in front of the gothic design, Connelly shifted from one foot to the other, and his hands trembled. He took a deep breath, rolled his shoulders, and the shaking ceased. Then he straightened like a soldier ready for combat, boldly pointed his Talisman finger, and shouted the incantation. "Sararta Morsmorde!"

Straight away, a thunderous noise grew overhead as dark smoky squares tumbled one by one and hung suspended in midair like large individual chalkboards. The conjured black squares descended and swelled against the walls, replacing them.

Then a misty giant blinked in and out like a light bulb blinking off and on, as it fought against the magic that was making it visible to the eye. Having lost its invisibility, an eight-foot, bulky and extremely muscular serpent covered in scaly blue skin, crawling with vermin, stood before a visible green swirling portal that was shaped like a giant cat's eye. Lima possessed the upper body of a man and the face of a cobra. At the end of two appendages were claw-like hands. Its eye slits held black oval balls with irises of yellow that were as twin flames of a lit candle. The black forked tongue darted in and out of fanged jaws, and when it hissed, it sounded like hot boiling steam from a locomotive.

Dr. Connelly inhaled the magic from his robe and stood firm in a fighting stance. Lima reared its head, shot it forward and blasted its breath. A stream of electricity bolted towards Dr. Connelly in a blur. It hit the shield causing Connelly to skid across the surface, but it didn't penetrate the armor. The second blast hoisted the shield high in the air and hurled it against the ceiling. After returning to ground, Connelly quickly cast the grounding spell that would bind the shield to a mystical surface. The demon reared back and blew a blast that thundered against the armor; the massive hit roared above it, but the shield held firm. The doctor countered with a spell that returned the demon's own fire. The returning blast knocked Lima backwards on its massive tail that acted as the curved legs on a giant rocker. It dazed Lima, but did little else.

The creature cut loose another blast; Connelly, pointing his Tomb Ring finger, countered with the same return-fire incantation, but the demon raised its tail and batted the bolt away, sending it flaming into midair. The creature fired on him at will; the bolts were coming too numerous and too forceful for the shield to hold. Connelly began to sweat profusely from the intense heat. The protective shield became an inferno. Lima seemed to sense the damage it had caused; it suddenly stopped and shot a thick, yellowish spit that covered the shield like crawling vomit. Dr. Connelly quickly incanted a spell and the shield rose; he crawled out from under it just in time, as the venom completely dissolved it in what seemed like seconds and left it a sticky pool of pale glue.

Connelly looked sadly at what was once his shield. The demon slithered in for the kill. The doctor waited for the drooling mouth to widen and flung a vial of Holy Water that splashed inside the massive jaws. He backed away as Lima tried in vain to use its breath and spit weapons. Enraged, Lima bared its fangs all the more and shot out six-inch claws. Dr. Connelly held the *Eye of the Cock* tightly in one hand and his dagger in the other. He stood firm as Lima wriggled forward. The nine-inch blade turned a fiery red, like a hot poker, and glowed. It extended itself far beyond its mere nine inches. The enchanted sword, now forty-eight inches, shot from Connelly's hand and swished through the air vertically, slashing off a deadly claw. Lima let out a loud hiss that was nearly deafening.

Connelly chanted in an unknown language. With every chant, the sword obeyed his command. Lima swung at the sword numerous times, but the sword darted back and forth, escaping all of Lima's attempts. The sword swished and darted all around Lima; with every slash, the demon lost energy and weakened. As it darted in again, Lima lunged forward and gulped the sword. Its saliva dissolved the magic metal and it was gone. Reaching a boiling point, its yellow flaming eyes danced rigorously within the oval balls as it moved forward to attack Connelly. But the Doctor had nowhere to run when Lima whipped its mighty claws horizontally through the air. Connelly leaped to one side, but not before getting raked across his left shoulder. "Aaarrh!" he yelled out in pain.

The sleeve hung shredded; blood trickled down his arm and dripped from the tips of his fingers. Appearing satisfied with the strike, the demon struck again like lightning and sank its fangs deep into Connelly, lifting him off the ground. It jarred the *Eye* and it slipped from his palm. High in the air, he gazed into the yellow flames of the beast. Lima held on to him, while its fangs pumped venom into his body. Dr. Connelly trembled from the effects of the poison like he was being cooked from the inside out. Without the power of the *Eye*, he was a dead man.

Slowly, with barely enough strength left, he gripped the last of his magical weapons from the bag that was tied around his waist. He tossed the twelve inch fangs in the air; they hit the ground as sparks and then rose as three giant Mongooses. They towered over Lima. Out-fanged and out-clawed, Lima dropped Dr. Connelly from its massive jaws. The three ferocious snake-fighters took turns ripping and biting the demon. They tore into Lima viciously, depleting Lima of precious energy which it needed to remain in the earth's realm.

*****

Steven watched helplessly as Esther struggled against the hands that held her firmly to the altar. Madame Reece stood over her with a ceremonial blade. She gripped it tightly with both hands and held it over Esther's heart. The black-cloaked crowd looked on gleefully with anticipation.

"Azi Dahaka Accio!" Madame commanded.

Suddenly a distant, deep hum permeated the air like a thousand drum rolls, and the floor shook ever so gently. Madame lost her concentration as the hum grew louder, and the floor shook more vigorously. Many in the crowd looked up and saw the hanging lamps swinging to and fro. Then small holes appeared, as if it punched out of the walls, and powdery concrete spilled through the openings like water leaking through cracks in a dam.

"What's happening?" a voice rose from the crowd.

The hum deepened into a loud rumble and the floor vibrated like a mini earthquake. Small pieces of ceiling fell like a light rain.

"The house is coming apart!" another shouted.

An eighty-year-old sorcerer closed her eyes and folded her hands over her chest as if she could sense something. "The sacred portal, it is closing," she said in a thick Hungarian accent.

"Madame, is that true?" asked a young follower.

"Impossible," Madame said, bewildered. "That mere idiot couldn't have possibly defeated Lima."

"Then it's true?" shouted another from the crowd.

"Go, Doc, go!" Steven yelled. He snatched away from the goons that had held him and stood cheering until his voice cracked.

The rumble grew to a near-deafening sound like the roar of a jet plane flying too low to the ground. By now, the floor was shaking violently and people fell over like duck pins, while others were crushed by large blocks of fallen stones, their screams rising above the roar. As massive stones fell and blocked stairwells, others were trampled to death when hundreds dashed for the few exits that remained. Madame Reece was abandoned; it was *every man for himself.* She rocked from side to side, unable to keep her balance. Esther, no longer held down, took advantage of the chaos, wobbled to her feet and reached for the dagger in Reece's hand.

"You bitch!" Esther shouted and pulled it from her.

She slammed her fist against Madame's nose, sending her thudding to the floor. Madame lay dazed until the floor cracked beneath her, opened and swallowed her. Her high-pitched scream drew little reaction from Esther and finally trailed off and was heard no more.

Esther ran over to Steven and saw he was out cold. A portion of the ceiling had fallen and cracked him on the head.

"Steve! Steve, get up!" She slapped him across the face several times until he lifted his head.

"Steve, come on. We've got to get out of here!"

After helping him to his feet, she grabbed his hand and the two made a mad dash for the stairwell. But he stopped.

"What the hell are you doing?" she said, shouting above the near-deafening rumble.

"Doc, we've got to find Doc!"

"No, Steve, we've got to get out of here!"

She grabbed Steven's hand again, and reluctantly he ran with her. The walls were falling in around them. They struggled to stay on their feet while stepping in blood and over dead bodies, away from live wiring and water main breaks. They choked on fumes from gas leaks, all the while ducking chunks of falling concrete. They tried desperately to maneuver around the cracks in the floor that were opening and gulping all in its path followed by screams as whole groups fell through. At the only remaining stairwell, Steven had to fight several followers before he and Esther could get through. Up ahead, Steven saw several people fall—all were trampled underfoot. The harsh push of the stampede broke his grip on Esther and she quickly disappeared in the large crowd of confusion.

"Esther!"

"Steve!"

He fought his way back up the stairwell; it was like running uphill into an avalanche. He kept his eyes on her head that was waving in and out of view. Several times their fingertips touched, only to be split apart by the maddened crowd. With all his might, he fought his way closer and closer to her.

Over the heads of the frantic human herd, Esther kept pointing to where he should meet her. Every time he pushed two steps towards her, the crowd pushed him five steps back. His main concern was not to fall. When he finally got her back in his sight, he pushed with every bit of strength he had until he reached the top of the stairs. But she had disappeared again. He looked around frantically, then saw her waiting near a large opening in the wall. He could see straight through it to the outside. He rushed over and saw that the opening was wide enough for them to squeeze through. He held on to her tightly as they stepped through the busted concrete. Steven felt the cool air upon his face and climbed out first, holding on to Esther. They managed to grab a large, thick tree branch. Each branch acted as steps on a ladder as they made their way down to the ground. As they looked around, there was no one else in sight. They ran as far as they could from the house.

Falling exhausted on the grass, they held one another as death screams filled the air and the once-tall castle-like mansion caved inward, crumbling into a large mass of cracked stones and sharp-edged steel. The dust of the massive stones rose like a thick gray cloud. Fire shot up like a rocket takeoff, and the thundering explosion ripped the sky. Steven shielded Esther with his body as debris and rain covered them like a dirty wet blanket.

"Doc," Steven said. His face cracked while looking at the giant pile of stones.

"I'm so sorry, Steve."

As soon as the building crumbled, the rain stopped, as if the two had a connection.

"Look!" Esther said, pointing to a rainbow. "I think God is telling us something," she said, half-smiling.

Steven never looked up. "I guess," he said.

Esther's smile fell as she looked at him.

"You were really fond of him, weren't you?"

"Crazy old man gave his life."

"I wish I had known him."

His eyes filled and he wiped his face on his jacket sleeve.

Noticing a small gash on his head, she tore a piece of her skirt and wiped the dirt from the wound. They sat on the wet grass holding each other. The night was quiet, and the moonlight made the crumbled stones glitter like a mountain of gold. The stars appeared to wink at them. Steven and Esther sat head to shoulder watching the sky. Tears and blood and dirt marked their faces.

"Did Madame Reece survive, you think?" Steven Asked.

"No. She's dead," she said unconcerned.

"I hope you're right."

"I saw her fall through the floor. You were unconscious."

She stood to leave, but Steven hesitated and stared at the massive pile. Finally, he followed her to the car. As they walked, he thought he saw a dark figure out of the corner of his eye. Esther turned and gasped.

"Oh my God!" she said, squeezing Steven's arm.

An exhausted Connelly limped from the shadows. His robe was half shredded. Its bold gold colors were now scarlet with his blood. Slightly bent over, he dragged a twisted leg behind him. His bare left arm dangled at his side, and in his right hand he gripped the *Eye of the Cock*. Connelly appeared to have aged twenty years. But to Steven he was beautiful. He ran to Connelly, nearly tipping the doctor over.

"Doc!"

Steven hugged Connelly, who went limp in his arms. He and Esther carried him to the car and laid him on the back seat. Esther drove like a speed demon to the nearest medical emergency.

*****

After Dr. Connelly and Steven spent a few days recovering in the hospital, the trio returned to Dayton and into the arms of their ecstatic loved ones. Esther revisited her faith. Dr. Connelly wrote a book on his battle with the dark forces and started his own lecture circuit. Steven kept in touch with him and even attended his book signings. The police never knew nor were they interested in the truth behind Madame Reece. They closed the book on Esther's kidnapping as solved.

But they dismissed the PPS as being just another cult and Reece as a nut case, blaming the destruction of the Kingston Hill Mansion, not on the portal's explosive closing, but on a gas leak.

After spending a short time apart, Esther and Steven became inseparable. One night they met for dinner at Kofi's, then took their favorite walk by the lake. They boarded the tour boat and stood looking out at the water.

"What were you and my mom talking about in the kitchen the other day?" Steven asked.

"Oh–girl talk," she said.

"No. Seriously. Mom had that look. Anything I should know?"

"I just asked her the same question I'd asked my own mom and got the same answer."

"What?"

"I asked how she and your dad managed to stay married for so many years, while most of my friends' parents were divorced."

"And she said?"

"She said that for many years, she and your dad were best friends first."

"Oh," he said.

Esther frowned when she saw that he felt the answer was no big deal. She turned to him and placed a palm on each side of his face.

"Steve, that's *us*."

He looked into her eyes and for the first time believed he saw love staring back at him. The thought of her loving him lit up his body just like the prayer had done before he attacked the guard. He pulled her against his chest; he parted his lips and took her mouth into his own. The wet warmth of her mouth made the ugliness of the whole world disappear. She pressed in and melted into his kiss.

A larger than normal raven flew overhead, then perched on a nearby branch overlooking the lake. It appeared to be observing the lovers as they sailed along the blue waters, looking up at the stars and the bright moonlight.

About the Author

H. L. Randall lives in Maryland and is a graduate of the University of Baltimore with degrees in English and Publications Design. Before launching a writing career, she worked for a private organization and taught Special Education in a Baltimore City public school. Aside from writing thrillers, poetry and romance, Ms. Randall is also one of the writers for the popular role playing game, *The Realm of Bethica.*

To learn more about Ms. Randall, you can go to her wbsite and web page below:

HLRandallbooks.com
theglasscateye.com

Please go to Amazon.com to leave a review of this book and to purchase other books by H. L. Randall.